Awful Ogre Running Wild

BY CHILDREN'S POET LAUREATE
JACK PRELUTSKY

ILLUSTRATIONS BY
PAUL O. ZELINSKY

Greenwillow Books
An Imprint of HarperCollins Publishers

For John Guth
—J. P.

For Sylvie and Virginia
—P. Z.

Awful Ogre Running Wild
Text copyright © 2008 by Jack Prelutsky
Illustrations copyright © 2008 by Paul O. Zelinsky
All rights reserved. Manufactured in China.
www.harpercollinschildrens.com

Watercolors and pen and ink were used to prepare the full-color art.
The text type is Cochin Bold.

Library of Congress Cataloging-in-Publication Data
Prelutsky, Jack.
Awful Ogre running wild / by Jack Prelutsky ;
illustrations by Paul O. Zelinsky.
p. cm.
"Greenwillow Books."
ISBN 978-0-06-623866-1 (trade bdg.) — ISBN 978-0-06-623867-8 (lib. bdg.)
[1. Ghouls and ogres—Juvenile poetry. 2. Children's poetry—American.
3. Ghouls and ogres—Poetry. 4. American poetry.] I. Zelinsky, Paul O., ill. II. Title.
PS3566.R36 A95 2008
811'.54 22   2007027683

First Edition 10 9 8 7 6 5 4 3 2 1

 Greenwillow Books

CONTENTS

AWFUL OGRE RUNS WILD

I'm running wild this morning,
I'm flinging pots of beans,
I'm heaving melons at the wall—
They burst to smithereens.
I pull apart my pillow,
I overturn my bed,
I swing my cudgel rampantly,
Then bang it on my head.

My pets are in a tizzy,
They scramble for the door,
As with my trusty battle-ax
I chop a bit of floor.
There hardly is a single thing
I do not decimate.
For summer is beginning,
And I thought I'd celebrate.

AWFUL OGRE EXERCISES

I'm doing calisthenics
With my awful ogre friends,
A bit of ogre yoga
And some massive deep knee bends.
We ride in place on bicycles
Until the pedals break,
Then bounce about on trampolines,
Which makes the building shake.

We toss around some boulders
Of enormous size and weight,
And then a dozen anvils,
And a stack of boiler plate.
We're rosy with exertion,
We grimace, gasp, and groan.
My friends all quit, they've had enough,
So now I'm on my own.

I hoist an anchor overhead—
It weighs a ton or two—
A feat not many ogres
Are strong enough to do.
There's nothing like a workout
At the Awful Ogre Gym. . . .
An ogre has to exercise
To keep himself in trim.

AWFUL OGRE SPEAKS OF TOAST

My toaster's out of order,
But I'm no knucklehead . . .
Until it's properly repaired,
A dragon toasts my bread.

AWFUL OGRE PAINTS A PICTURE

I wear my red bandanna
And my favorite beret.
I'm about to paint a picture
And prefer to dress this way.
There is paint upon my palette,
Not too little, not too much,
And the canvas on my easel
Now awaits my brush's touch.

I'll portray my rats in togas
And I'll give them double chins.
I'll paint them wearing silly hats
And playing violins.
I'll add a vivid background
Of assorted gaudy slime.
It's sure to be a masterpiece,
And utterly sublime.

I'm filled with inspiration,
Almost more than I can bear.
I'm adding nameless creatures
With enormous mops of hair.
Perhaps I'll add my rattlesnake,
My faithful buzzard, too. . . .
I am an awful ogre,
And an artist through and through.

AWFUL OGRE'S PICNIC

We're having a picnic,
My ogress and I.
The grass has turned yellow,
Clouds darken the sky.
We lunch on a platter
Of lizard-stuffed skunk
And razor-thin slices
Of mastodon trunk.

We overturn rocks
To exasperate bugs,
We startle some spiders
And juggle some slugs.
We sing a duet
In melodious tones,
Then buffet each other
With branches and stones.

We clamber up boulders
And shinny up trees,
We laugh as we're stung
By a squadron of bees.
We tromp in the mud
And we slosh in the swamp,
Then wrestle with crocodiles
Just for a romp.

I gather dead flowers,
A present for her,
The thorniest ones,
Which she seems to prefer.
We finish our lunch
With some turtle-shell pie. . . .
We're having a picnic,
My ogress and I.

AWFUL OGRE ENTERS A COOK-OFF

Today's the Ogre Cook-off,
It's an annual event,
And I've prepared a specialty,
Extremely succulent.
I've been entering this contest
For a hundred years or more.
It's been very disappointing,
For I've never won before.

I took honorable mention
Less than fifty years ago
With my curdled gerbil burger
Stuffed with bits of buffalo.
But I know that I'm competing
Against all my ogre aunts,
So I cannot help but wonder
If I have the slightest chance.

There are many other entrants,
With assorted smelly stews,
Abominable casseroles,
And moldy cheese fondues.
I see scores of preparations
Making use of sludge and slime. . . .
Will my little dish be noticed?
Am I merely wasting time?

I cross my fingers hopefully
And make a silent wish,
As the awful ogre judges
Sample every single dish.
Then I hear a loud announcement:
"Awful Ogre, you have won!"
And the other ogres cheer me
In resounding unison.

I am filled with such emotion
That I simply cannot speak.
A tear appears inside my eye
And trickles down my cheek.
Now I wear a big blue ribbon
For my cactus bat brochette,
And they even took my picture
For the *Ogres' Home Gazette.*

AWFUL OGRE ATTENDS A CONCERT

We're dressed in our best
And we're down at the mall,
Attending a concert
At Ogresong Hall.
My favorite trio
Is set to appear:
Oregano Ogres!
I clap and I cheer.

They open with standards
All ogres adore,
"Stomp Stomping through Swampland"
And "Oceans of Gore."
They then thrill us all
With their platinum hits,
"A Bush Full of Needles"
And "Writhing in Pits."

They roll in a puddle
Of mud on the stage,
They smash their guitars
As they bellow and rage.
Their voices are deafening,
Weird, and bizarre . . .
The louder they clamor,
The better they are.

Their singular show
Is about to conclude,
They shower the crowd
With inedible food.
We roar as they give
One another a bite—
I so love a concert
On Saturday night.

AWFUL OGRE PAYS A VISIT

I'm visiting Grandmother Ogress today,
She brews us hot griffin-beak tea.
She's lively and spry, though she's ancient and gray . . .
She's two thousand seventy-three.

She loves to complain of her aches and her pains,
Yet while she's complaining, she'll grin.
She feeds me a snack of dried weasel remains
And tickles me under my chin.

She hands me a sandwich of manticore tongue
On slices of moldy old bread.
She tells me wild stories of when she was young
And tenderly touches my head.

She boasts how she bested a goblin or two,
Then shows me a souvenir claw.
She serves me a bowlful of dragon-scale stew
And gives me a kiss on the jaw.

She's incontrovertibly one of a sort
And head of my whole ogre clan.
I hug her good-bye, and she lets out a snort—
I visit whenever I can.

AWFUL OGRE SPEAKS OF TRANSPORTATION

If I could ride a horse, I would,
But horses are too small,
And when I mount an elephant,
It tends to trip and fall.

Some dinosaurs were large enough,
Alas, they are no more.
So I'm obliged to walk a lot—
That's why my feet are sore.

AWFUL OGRE ALL ALONE

I'm atop Old Ogre Mountain,
And I'm gazing all around.
Clouds are floating far below me.
I can't hear a single sound.
Birds are nowhere in attendance,
They could never fly this high,
So there's nothing to disturb me
As I almost scrape the sky.

Here upon the very apex
Of this monumental hill,
I'm contented, calm, and peaceful,
And I'm sitting very still.
Though it took a while to get here,
It was clearly worth the climb—
On occasion, even ogres
Need a little quiet time.

AWFUL OGRE
CAUSES A COMMOTION

The forest quaked and trembled,
And the goblins shrieked and fled.
The elves were in a panic,
And the trolls rolled out of bed.

My buzzard shed some feathers,
And the gnomes fell to their knees,
And all because this afternoon
I sneezed a single sneeze.

AWFUL OGRE SWIMS

On sweltering days
I am utterly fond
Of taking a dip
In the neighborhood pond.
I bring my piranha—
It's special for him.
We dive in together
And merrily swim.

We splash and we splish
With exuberant glee.
The pond has no fish,
So he nibbles on me.
There's nothing like swimming
When summer's too hot. . . .
Piranhas and ogres
Love water a lot.

AWFUL OGRE AND THE ANIMALS

A porcupine shed all its quills,
A moose stood on its head.
A walrus climbed a palm tree,
A rhinoceros played dead.
The parrots lost their voices,
And the swans began to sing.
The mountain goats all stumbled,
And a chimp fell off its swing.

The tigers cringed in terror,
And the lions slunk away.
The elephants turned somersaults,
Then hid behind their hay.
A hippo started hopping
Like an addled kangaroo—
There's always some excitement
When I drop in at the zoo.

AWFUL OGRE
STAYS AT AN INN

I'm staying for the weekend
At a little inn I know.
When I'm a trifle moody,
It's where I often go.
I need no reservations,
My hosts have made this clear.
The other guests all vanish
As soon as I appear.

My room is always ready
And furnished to my taste,
Including dainty paintings
Of glowing toxic waste.
Bats dangle from the ceiling,
Bugs crawl on every wall,
The shower water's rusty
When the shower works at all.

Sometimes my room is stuffy,
Sometimes it's icy cold.
The corners harbor spiders
Concealed by webs and mold.
The bedding is disheveled,
They do not change it much,
And something on my pillow
Is slimy to the touch.

The mattress is too lumpy,
The springs are old and worn.
The windows are all grimy,
The curtains are all torn.
The carpets are in tatters
And have a musty smell.
I always feel at home here . . .
It's a wonderful hotel.

AWFUL OGRE GOES DRAGON-WATCHING

Today's a dragon-watching day,
I'm wedged in a ravine,
In hopes I'll spy a specimen
No ogre's ever seen.
I focus my monocular,
Then check my master list
Of dragons that I've yet to spot . . .
A few may not exist.

Emerging from the underbrush,
A Yellowneck appears.
I pay it scant attention,
I've observed them many years.
A pair of Dreary Greenheads
Are the next I chance to see.
They're common in the neighborhood,
And do not interest me.

I note a Speckled Bumpyback,
And mutter in disgust.
It's awkward, unattractive,
And ubiquitous as dust.
I feel a bit discouraged
And my bottom's getting sore.
The dragons that I've seen so far
I've often seen before.

But suddenly I hold my breath . . .
I can't believe my eye.
A Ruby-crested Goldenside
Is gliding through the sky!
Of all the dragons ever,
It's the rarest of the rare.
I marvel as it pirouettes,
Then hovers in the air.

The sunlight brightly glistens
On its iridescent scales.
Its eyes are silver lanterns,
It has seven silken tails.
I'm filled with wordless wonder
As it slowly soars away. . . .
It's been a most exhilarating
Dragon-watching day.